LIEUTENANT
KIZHE

YURI TYNIANOV

LIEUTENANT KIZHE

A novella

Translated by Nicolas Pasternak Slater

Illustrations by Olga Smart

Look MultiMedia
lookmm.com

Look MultiMedia

Translated by Nicolas Pasternak Slater from
Подпоручик Киже (Podporuchik Kizhe)

First published in the USSR 1927

This translation published by Look Multimedia Ltd 2021

ISBN 978-1-9999815-6-3

Look Multimedia Ltd
14 Penn Road
London N7 9RD
United Kingdom

www.lookmm.com

Typeset in Sabon 10½pt by
www.chandlerbookdesign.co.uk

Printed in Great Britain by
TJ Books Ltd, Padstow, Cornwall

INTRODUCTION

Yuri Tynianov was born in 1894 to a well-to-do provincial Jewish family in what is now Latvia. From 1912 he studied literature at Petersburg University, showing a particular interest in Pushkin. Nine years later he was appointed professor of Russian literature at the Institute of Art History in Petrograd. He was at various times a literary theorist and campaigner, literary critic, novelist and short story writer, film director, mimic and impersonator. With his mischievous and ironic sense of humour (which bursts through in many of his writings) he was a natural satirist, and *Lieutenant Kizhe* is a delicious example of his skill.

The story relates to Russia under Tsar Pavel (or Paul) the First, the son of Catherine the Great. Pavel bitterly resented his mother, and on ascending the throne reversed many of her policies, dismissed her appointees, and installed rigidly disciplinarian, autocratic regulations in the Prussian style. His reforms

1

were unpopular, and he was assassinated less than five years after accession.

The tale of a non-existent personage, created by a slip of the pen in a blindly bureaucratic society and taking on a life of his own, is something of a classic trope. Tynianov's account of Lieutenant Kizhe is purportedly based on an actual event during Pavel's reign. Tynianov will have been aware of similar real-life events in more recent history, and could see how the increasingly authoritarian character of the Bolshevik bureaucracy exposed it to this kind of mockery. The story has given rise to two films and a ballet (with music by Prokofiev).

Though fictitious, the story is solidly founded on history. Many named characters, major and minor, are genuine (including the influential Baron Arakcheyev, a ruthless military martinet whom Pavel favoured). Even Count Pahlen, one of the leading conspirators in Pavel's assassination, has a walk-on part in the story.

Nicolas Pasternak Slater is a retired medical specialist who has been translating Russian literature since the 1990s. He has published translations of Boris Pasternak (including *Doctor Zhivago*), Turgenev (including *Fathers and Sons*), Pushkin, Tolstoy, Dostoevsky (including *Crime and Punishment*), Chekhov, Teffi, and the modern writers Osipov and Movshevich.

Tsar Pavel was dozing by his open window. During the hour after dinner, when food fights its slow battle with the body, all interruptions were forbidden. He dozed, seated in his tall armchair, enclosed at the back and on either side by a glass screen. Tsar Pavel Petrovich was dreaming his usual postprandial dream.

He dreamt he was at Gatchina, sitting in his well-tended garden, and the plump Cupid in the corner was watching him eat dinner with his family. There was a distant screeching sound, which approached closer and closer along the rutted track, jolting up and down as it came. Pavel Petrovich caught sight of a triangular shape in the distance, galloping horses, a curricle on its way, dust. He hid under the table, because that triangle was a State courier. Someone was galloping from Petersburg to find him.

"Nous sommes perdus…" he cried out hoarsely to his wife from under the table, meaning her to hide too.

But there wasn't enough air under the table, and the screeching was right here, and the curricle's shafts were coming at him.

The State courier glanced under the table, found Pavel Petrovich, and said:

"Your Majesty. Her Majesty your mother has died."

But as soon as Pavel Petrovich started clambering out from under the table, the courier clipped him over the forehead and shouted: "Guards!"

Pavel Petrovich flapped him away, and trapped a fly.

And now, there he sat, staring wide-eyed out of the window of the Pavlovsky Palace, gasping from his food, gasping with misery, with the fly buzzing in his hand, and listened.

Beneath his window, someone had shouted "Guards!"

2

In the offices of the Preobrazhensky Regiment, an army clerk had been exiled to Siberia as a punishment.

The replacement clerk, still a young lad, was sitting at his desk writing. His hand was shaking, because he was running late.

He was supposed to finish copying out the regimental order by six o'clock precisely, for the duty adjutant to deliver it to the palace, where His Majesty's adjutant would attach it to other similar orders and present them to the Tsar at nine. Lateness was a crime. The regimental clerk had got up extra early, but had spoilt the order and now he was making a fresh copy. In his first copy he had made two mistakes: he had listed Lieutenant Sinyukhayev as dead, because Sinyukhayev had followed immediately after Major Sokolov who had indeed died; and he had made an absurd slip of the pen: instead of writing 'The Ensigns above: Steven, Rybin and Azancheyev, are appointed...', he had written 'Ensign Above, Steven, Rybin and Azancheyev, are appointed'. In Russian this came out as: 'Ensign Kizhe, Steven, Rybin and Azancheyev...' While he was writing the word '*Ensigns*', an officer had come in, and he had stood to attention, breaking off on the last letter of 'Ensign'; and on sitting down to work again, he got mixed up and wrote '*Ensign Kizhe*'.

He knew that if the order wasn't ready by six, the adjutant would shout 'Take him!' and he'd be arrested. That was why his hand wasn't working properly, he was writing slower and slower, and suddenly he splashed a great big ink-blot, elegant as a fountain, over the order.

He had only ten minutes left.

Throwing himself back in his seat, the clerk looked at the clock, as if it were a living person; then his fingers, moving as though separate from his body and acting of their own volition, started scrabbling among the papers to find a blank sheet, although there wasn't a single blank sheet there – they were all in the cupboard, stacked nice and neatly in a pile.

But as he sat there in abject despair, scrabbling away to no purpose save to preserve the last shreds of his self-respect, he froze in horror yet again.

Another paper, no less important than the first, had a mistake in it too.

According to the Imperial Addendum to No.940, concerning the avoidance of certain terms in official reports, one was not supposed to use the word 'check', but *'review'*; not 'carry out', but *'execute'*; not 'sentries' but *'guards'*, and on no account to write the word 'squad', but *'detachment'*.

For civilian documents there were additional provisions: not to write 'degree' but *'class'*, not 'society' but *'association'*; and instead of the word 'citizen', to use *'merchant'* or *'tradesman'*.

But all this was written in tiny handwriting, at the bottom of Instruction No.940, which was hanging on the wall right here, before the clerk's own eyes; he hadn't read it, but had learned all about 'checking' and the rest of it on his very first day, and remembered it perfectly.

And yet the paper drawn up for the regimental commander's signature, before being delivered to Baron Arakcheyev, contained the words:

'Having *checked*, according to your Excellency's instructions, the *squads* of *sentries* detailed for service within the city of Saint Petersburg and beyond its limits, I have the honour to report that all of the above has been *carried out*.'

And even that wasn't all.

The first line of the report that he himself had just copied out, read as follows:

Your Excellency, Dear Sir.

The merest child would have known perfectly well that a salutation occupying a single line indicated an order; whereas reports from an inferior, particularly when addressed to such a personage as Baron Arakcheyev, had to have the salutation written on two lines, thus:

Your Excellency
Dear Sir,

indicating subordination and courtesy.

And even if the words *checked,* and all the rest, might have been put down to his not having noticed the instruction or attended to it in good time, the *Dear Sir* was a solecism for which he alone was responsible.

And the clerk, no longer knowing what he was doing, sat down to correct that paper. As he copied it, he instantly forgot about the regimental order, though that was much more pressing.

When the adjutant's messenger arrived to pick up the order, the clerk looked at the clock, and at the messenger, and at once passed him the page with the deceased Lieutenant Sinyukhayev on it.

After which, still trembling, he sat down again and wrote the words *Excellency* and *detachments* and *guard.*

3

At nine o'clock precisely, a bell rang in the palace. The Tsar had pulled the bell-rope. And at nine o'clock precisely, His Majesty's adjutant entered with the report for Tsar Pavel Petrovich. Pavel Petrovich was seated in the same place as yesterday, by the window, with the glass screen round him.

But this time he was not asleep or dozing, and his face wore a different expression.

The adjutant, like everyone else in the palace, knew that the Tsar was angry. But he knew just as certainly that this anger was looking for reasons, and the more reasons it found, the hotter it would burn. So the report must not on any account be left out.

He drew himself up in front of the glass screen, behind the Tsar's back, and announced himself.

Pavel Petrovich did not turn to look at him. He drew scanty, laboured breaths.

Throughout the whole of the previous day, people had tried and failed to discover who had shouted out "Guards!" beneath his window. And that night he had twice woken in fear.

"Guards!" had been an absurd thing to shout, and to start with Pavel Petrovich's anger had just been mild, as anyone would have been angry if he had been having a bad dream and been prevented from seeing it through to the end. Because a happy ending to a dream does, after all, mean happiness. And also he was curious: who had called out "Guards!" right under his window, and why? But when the whole palace, in abject terror, had been unable to find that person, the Tsar's anger had grown great. What it all meant was that in this very palace, after dinner, someone had succeeded in causing unrest, and yet could not be found. And at the same time no one had any idea what the reason had been for shouting "Guards!" Perhaps it had been a warning from some repentant malefactor.

Or perhaps, out there among the bushes which had been searched three times over, someone had shoved a gag into the man's mouth and choked him. He seemed to have vanished from the face of the earth.

They would have to... But what had to be done, if that man wasn't found?

They would have to reinforce the patrols. And not just here, either.

Pavel Petrovich, still not turning round, stared out at the rectangular green bushes, almost the same as the ones at the Trianon. They had been clipped. And yet there was no telling who was hiding in them.

Without looking at the adjutant, he held out his right hand behind him. The adjutant knew what this meant. At times of great anger, the Tsar does not turn round. Deftly he handed over the order about the Preobrazhensky Guards Regiment, and Pavel Petrovich began to read it attentively. Then the arm was extended backwards once more, and the adjutant, guessing what was wanted, soundlessly picked up a pen from the little desk, dipped it in the inkwell, shook it and laid it gently onto that hand, smudging himself with ink as he did so. All this took only a moment. The paper was briskly signed and tossed back at the adjutant. And the adjutant went on handing over page after page, and the pages, now signed or just read over, flew back at him one after the other. He was getting quite used to this activity, and was hoping it would all pass without trouble, when the

Tsar leaped up from his raised chair.

Taking tiny steps, he ran up to the adjutant. His face was red, his eyes dark. He walked right up to the adjutant and sniffed at him. That was what the Tsar did when he was suspicious. Then he firmly seized the adjutant's sleeve between two fingers and pinched him.

The adjutant stood erect, holding the sheets of paper in his hand.

"You don't know your duty, my man," said Pavel hoarsely. "Coming at me from behind."

And he pinched him again.

"I'll flog that Potemkin spirit out of you. Dismiss."

And the adjutant backed out through the doorway.

No sooner had the door been noiselessly closed than Pavel hastily untied his neckcloth and began silently tearing at his shirt-front; his mouth twisted, and his lips began to tremble.

He was working up a serious rage.

4

Before signing the order for the Preobrazhensky Guards regiment, the Tsar had angrily amended it. He had corrected the words 'Ensign Kizhe, Steven, Rybin and Azancheyev', inserting a huge hard-sign where it was missing after the word 'Ensign', and striking out a number of letters that followed it. And above that he had written 'Ensign Kizhe to guard duty'. Apart from that he had raised no objections. The order was handed over.

When the commanding officer received it, he spent a long time trying to remember who this ensign was, with the strange surname of Kizhe. He immediately got out the list of all the officers in the Preobrazhensky regiment, but there was no officer of that name. The name did not even appear among the other ranks.

He couldn't understand what was going on. The only man in all the world who did understand was a certain clerk, but nobody asked him, and he told nobody. However, the Tsar's order had to be obeyed. And yet it could not be obeyed because there was no ensign Kizhe in the whole regiment.

The commanding officer wondered whether he should consult Baron Arakcheyev. But he quickly gave up that idea. Baron Arakcheyev lived at Gatchina; and in any case there was no saying what would happen.

In any disastrous situation, the accepted thing to do was to consult one's relatives; so the commanding officer immediately decided that he was related to His Majesty's adjutant Sablukov, and galloped off to Pavlovskoye.

At Pavlovskoye everything was in great confusion, and at first the adjutant wouldn't receive the commanding officer.

Then he listened to him with distaste, and was about to send him packing, for he had plenty to do without all this; but suddenly he knitted his brows, cast a glance at the commanding officer, and his expression changed. A reckless look came into his eyes.

Slowly the adjutant said:

"Don't report this to the Tsar. Consider this Ensign Kizhe as a living person. Appoint him to the guard."

And without another glance at the commanding officer, who had gone limp with horror, he abandoned him to his fate. He drew himself up and walked away.

5

Lieutenant Sinyukhayev was a scruffy lieutenant. His father had been a medical officer under Baron Arakcheyev, who, as a reward for the pills that had restored him to health, had quietly got the doctor's son a place in the regiment. The baron had liked the son's straightforward, unintelligent appearance. In the regiment, he had no particular friends, but nor did he avoid his fellow officers. He was taciturn, liked his tobacco, had no dealings with women, and (though this was no occupation for a proper officer), he enjoyed playing the oboe d'amore.

His kit was always kept smart.

When the regimental order was read out, Sinyukhayev was standing rigidly to attention as usual, and not thinking about anything.

Suddenly he heard his own name read out, and his ears twitched like a horse's when it is lost in thought and unexpectedly feels the whip.

"Lieutenant Sinyukhayev, having died of a fever, is considered to have left the service."

At this point the commanding officer, who was reading the order, unconsciously looked at the place where Sinyukhayev always stood; and the hand that held the sheet of paper was lowered.

Sinyukhayev was standing in his place as he always did. But presently the commanding officer went on reading the order – admittedly not as crisply as before – and read the passage about Steven, Azancheyev, and Kizhe. And read to the end. The men began to disperse, and Sinyukhayev ought to have gone out to practise drill movements. But instead of going out, he remained standing still.

He had become used to hearing the words of the regimental order as words of a special kind, not resembling human speech. They did not possess sense or meaning; what they had was a life and power of their own. It didn't matter whether an order was carried out or not; orders somehow changed regiments, streets and people, even if they weren't carried out.

When he heard the words of the order, he at first remained standing still, like someone who hadn't heard what was said. He tried to grasp the words. And then he no longer had any doubt.

It was about him. And when his column moved off, he began to wonder whether he was really alive.

He could feel his hand resting on his sword-hilt, and a certain tightness of the straps of his sword-belt, and the weight of his pigtail which he had greased that morning, and all this seemed to indicate that he was alive; but at the same time he knew that there was something wrong here, something had been irredeemably spoiled. Not for an instant did he think that there could be a mistake in the order.

On the contrary, it seemed to him that the mistake, the blunder, lay in his being alive. It was his carelessness that had prevented him from noticing, and letting people know.

In any case, he was getting in the way of all the drill exercises by standing stock still on the parade-ground. And yet it never occurred to him to move a muscle.

As soon as the parade was over, the commander flew at the lieutenant, crimson-faced. It was really lucky that owing to the hot weather the Tsar had not attended the parade, but was resting at Pavlovskoye. The commander was about to bellow "Report to the guard-room", but to vent his fury properly he needed something more resonant, and he was preparing to roll his R's and shout "Arr-rr-rrest that man!" when suddenly his mouth snapped shut as though it had just trapped a fly. And there he stood, confronting Lieutenant Sinyukhayev, for some two minutes.

Then he recoiled from him as though this man had the plague, and marched off.

He had remembered that Lieutenant Sinyukhayev, being dead, had been dismissed from the service; and he had restrained himself because he had no idea how to address such a person.

6

Tsar Pavel Petrovich was pacing back and forth in his room, pausing from time to time.

He was listening.

Ever since the day when the Tsar, in his travelling cloak and dusty riding-boots, had clattered through the room with ringing spurs – the room in which his mother was still snoring – and slammed the door shut, people had observed that that a great anger would grow into a gigantic anger, and the gigantic anger would end two days later in terror and sentimentality.

The monsters on the staircases at Pavlovskoye had been created by the wild Brenna, while the palace ceilings and walls were done by Cameron, a lover of delicate colours that melt before your gaze.

On the one hand the gaping maws of rampant, human-like lions; on the other – elegant sensibility.

What was more, there were two lanterns hanging in the palace hall, gifts from the recently beheaded Louis XVI. These gifts he had received in France, when he was still travelling under the name of Count Severny.

The lanterns were of exquisite workmanship, with panels so constructed that they softened the light they gave.

But Pavel Petrovich avoided lighting them.

And there was a clock, a gift from Marie-Antoinette, standing on a jasper table. The hour hand was a gold Saturn with a long pigtail, the minute hand a cherub holding an arrow.

When the clock struck midday or midnight, Saturn's pigtail hid the cherub's arrow.

That signified that time vanquishes love.

However that might be, the clock was never wound.

And so, there was Brenna in the garden, Cameron on the walls, and overhead, in the empty space below the ceiling, there dangled Louis XVI's lantern.

At the times of his great anger, Pavel Petrovich actually acquired a superficial resemblance to one of Brenna's lions.

At such times, like a storm out of a clear sky, whole regiments would be beaten with staves; far away on the Don, at dead of night, someone's head would be cut off by torchlight; and random soldiers, clerks, lieutenants, generals and governors-general would be marched off on foot to Siberia.

The usurper of the throne, his mother, was dead. He had crushed the spirit of Potemkin, as Ivan the Fourth had once crushed the spirit of the boyars. He had scattered Potemkin's bones and razed his tomb. He had annihilated his mother's very taste. A usurper's taste! The gold, the rooms lined with Indian silk, the rooms filled with Chinese porcelain, with their Dutch stoves, the room of blue glass... A snuff-box. A travelling fairground. The Roman and Greek medals she was so proud of! He gave orders for them to be used to gild his palace.

And yet that spirit survived, the taste of it persisted.

The smell of it was all around him; that might have been why Pavel Petrovich habitually sniffed at his interlocutors.

And overhead, like a hanged Frenchman, dangled the lantern.

Terror overcame the Tsar. He gasped for air. He feared neither his wife nor his elder sons, any of whom

– recalling the example of a merry grandmother and mother-in-law – might stab him to death with a fork and mount the throne.

He did not fear his suspiciously cheerful ministers, nor his suspiciously gloomy generals. He did not even fear any of that fifty-million-strong rabble who sat out there on the hillocks, swamps, sands and fields of his empire, and whom he simply could not imagine. He did not fear them, taken individually. But taken together they were an ocean, and he was drowning in it.

So he had his Petersburg fortress surrounded by moats and protected by guard-posts, and set up a drawbridge hoisted on chains. But even the chains couldn't be trusted – they were guarded by sentries.

Amd when the great anger turned to a great terror, the Criminal Affairs office set to work, and one man was strung up by his arms, and another felt the floor give way under him, and down below the masters of the executioner's trade were waiting.

And so, when short little steps were heard coming from the Tsar's room, and longer ones, and sudden stumbles, everyone exchanged anxious glances, and not many smiled. The great terror was in that room.

The Tsar was pacing up and down.

7

Lieutenant Sinyukhayev was standing on the very spot where his commanding officer had flown at him to tear him to pieces, and had not torn him, and had stopped so suddenly.

There was not a soul about.

As a rule, at the end of the parade, he would relax, ease off his body, loosen up his arms, and walk away to the barracks with an easy gait. All his limbs regained their freedom; he became a civilian again.

Back home, in the officers' quarters, he would unbutton his tunic and play the oboe d'amore. Then he would fill his pipe and gaze out of the window. He could see a wide stretch of the treeless garden, now turned into a waste-ground known as Tsarina's Field. It was a field with no variety and no greenery, but the sandy ground preserved the prints of horses and soldiers. He enjoyed every stage of his smoking: filling, tamping down, drawing, and the smoke itself. So long as a man can smoke, nothing can hurt him. That was all he needed; soon the evening would fall, and he would go and join his fellow officers, or just go for a walk.

He enjoyed the courtesy of the common people. A merchant had once said to him, when he sneezed, "May God bless you, Sir!"

Before going to sleep he would play cards with his batman. He had taught the man to play Kontra and Pamfil, and when the batman lost, the lieutenant would tap him on the nose with the pack of cards, but when he lost himself, he didn't tap the man. Finally he would inspect the kit that his batman had cleaned, curl, plait and grease his pigtail himself, and go to bed.

But this time he did not stretch himself, his muscles were tense, and no breath could be heard passing through his lips. He looked over the parade-ground, and it seemed unfamiliar to him. At least, he had never before noticed the cornices over the windows of the red-brick barrack building, nor its grubby windows.

The round cobblestones of the parade-ground were as different as unlike brothers.

Neat and tidy in its grey uniformity, soldierlike St. Petersburg lay before him, with its waste grounds, rivers, and the dull eyes of its pavements: an utterly unfamiliar town to him.

Then he understood that he had died.

8

Pavel Petrovich heard the footsteps of the adjutant who had crept cat-like up to his chair behind its glass screen, and sat down as firmly as if he had been sitting all along.

He knew the footsteps of those who came up to him. Sitting with his back to them, he could tell the scraping steps of the confident ones, the hopping of the flatterers, and the light, airy steps of the terrified ones.

He never heard straight and ordinary steps.

On this occasion the adjutant was walking confidently, scraping his soles. Pavel Petrovich half-turned his head.

The adjutant came up to the middle of the screen and bowed his head.

"Your Majesty. The man who shouted for the guards was Ensign Kizhe."

"Who's he?"

His terror eased: he was being given a name. The adjutant hadn't been expecting the question and took a step backwards.

"An ensign assigned to guard duty, Your Majesty."

"What did he shout for?" The Tsar tapped his foot on the floor. "I'm listening, sir."

The adjutant hesitated a moment.

"Stupidity, sire," he stammered.

"Set up an inquiry, have him flogged and marched off to Siberia."

9

So began the life of Ensign Kizhe.

When the clerk was copying the order, Ensign Kizhe was an error, a slip of the pen, no more than that. The error might never have been noticed, and it would have sunk beneath a sea of paper; and since there was nothing interesting about the order, later historians would probably never even have quoted it.

But Pavel Petrovich's carping eye had singled it out, and by adding a hard-sign had conferred a questionable life on it. The slip of the pen had become an ensign with no face, but with a surname.

Then the adjutant's faltering thoughts had created a face for him: a face that barely glimmered, it is true: like one in a dream. It was he who had shouted "Guards!" under the palace window.

Now this face had hardened and filled out: Ensign Kizhe had turned out to be a malefactor, condemned to be flogged on the block, or at best over a vaulting-horse – and then Siberia.

This was reality.

Up till now he had been a clerk's anxiety, a commander's distraction, and an adjutant's inventiveness.

Now the vaulting-horse, the lashes and the journey to Siberia were his own personal affair.

The order had to be executed. Ensign Kizhe had to leave the military world, enter the judicial world, and then take the green path straight to Siberia.

And that was what happened.

The commanding officer of the regiment to which he belonged, standing in front of his troops on parade, yelled out the name of Ensign Kizhe in a thunderous voice such as one only ever hears from a man who is utterly lost.

The vaulting-horse was already positioned to one side, and two guardsmen had looped leather straps about it at the head and tail ends. The two guardsmen, one on either side, each holding a cat-o'-nine-tails, whipped the smooth wood, while a third one counted the lashes, and the regiment looked on.

Since the wood had already been polished smooth by thousands of bellies, the vaulting-horse did not appear to be quite empty. Although there was no one on it, in a way it still seemed as if there was someone. The soldiers puckered their brows and looked at the silent horse, and when the flogging was done the commanding officer went red in the face and flared his nostrils, as he always did.

Then the straps were undone; and it was as if someone's shoulders had been released from the horse. Two guardsmen approached and awaited a word of command.

Leaving the regiment behind, they marched off along the road at a steady pace, rifles at the slope, casting occasional sideways glances not at each other but at the gap between them.

Among the ranks there stood a young shaven-headed soldier, only recently enlisted. He watched the flogging with interest. He thought that everything that was happening was an everyday occurrence, something often done in military service.

But that evening he suddenly turned over on his bunk and quietly asked the old guardsman who lay beside him:

"Uncle, who's our Tsar?"

"Pavel Petrovich, you fool," replied the older man in alarm.

"Have you ever seen him?"

"Yes, I have," barked the old man, "and you'll see him too."

They fell silent. But the old soldier couldn't get to sleep. He kept turning over. Ten minutes went by.

"Why did you ask that?" the older man suddenly asked the young one.

"Well, I don't know," the young man readily replied. "They keep going on about the Tsar, but who is he – who knows? Maybe it's all just talk…"

"Idiot," said the old man, squinting this way and that. "Belt up, you country bumpkin."

Another ten minutes passed. In the barracks all was dark and quiet.

"He does exist," the old man suddenly whispered in the young man's ear. "Only he's a fake."

10

Lieutenant Sinyukhayev looked attentively round the room he had inhabited till that day.

It was a spacious room with a low ceiling, and on the wall was the portrait of a middle-aged man wearing spectacles and a small pigtail. This was the lieutenant's father, Doctor Sinyukhayev.

He lived at Gatchina; but looking at the portrait, the lieutenant didn't feel particularly confident of that. Perhaps he did live there, perhaps he didn't.

Then he looked at the objects that had belonged to Lieutenant Sinyukhayev: the oboe d'amore in its wooden case, the tongs for curling his wig, the jar of powder, the sand-box; and all these objects looked back at him. He averted his eyes.

There he stood, in the middle of the room, awaiting something. Not his batman, for sure.

But it was the batman who cautiously entered the room and stopped in front of the lieutenant. He opened his mouth a little, looked at the lieutenant, and stood there.

Probably he always stood like that when waiting for orders; but the lieutenant looked at him as if he was seeing him for the first time, and lowered his eyes.

Death had to be hushed up for a while, like a crime. That evening a young man came into his room, sat down at the desk where the oboe d'amore lay in its box, took the oboe out and blew into it; failing to produce any sound, he put it aside in a corner.

Then he called for the batman and told him to bring some vodka. Not once did he look at Lieutenant Sinyukhayev.

But the lieutenant asked, in a strained voice:

"Who are you?"

The young man, as he drank his vodka, answered with a yawn:

"Senate auditor, Officer cadets' school." And he ordered the batman to make the bed. Then he started undressing, and Lieutenant Sinyukhayev spent a long time admiring how neatly the auditor pulled off his half-boots and clattered them to one side onto the floor, unbuttoned his clothes, covered himself with a blanket and yawned. Finally he stretched out, then suddenly looked at Lieutenant Sinyukhayev's sleeve, and pulled out a linen handkerchief from the the turned-up cuff. He blew his nose, and yawned once more.

And now, at last, Lieutenant Sinyukhayev pulled himself together and said listlessly that this was against regulations.

The auditor unconcernedly replied that on the contrary, it was all in accordance with regulations; that he was acting under Section 2, since the erstwhile Sinyukhayev was 'apparently deceased'; and he told the lieutenant to take off his uniform, which appeared to the auditor to be still in a decent condition, and to put on another uniform which was no longer serviceable.

Lieutenant Sinyukhayev began taking off his uniform, and the auditor helped him, explaining that the erstwhile Sinyukhayev 'might not do it right'.

Then the erstwhile Sinyukhayev put on the uniform that was no longer serviceable, and stood there, fearing that the auditor might take his gloves. He had a pair of long yellow gloves, uniform gloves with seamed fingers. Losing one's gloves, he had heard, was dishonourable. With gloves on, a lieutenant – no matter how he looked – was still a lieutenant. And so the erstwhile Sinyukhayev pulled on his gloves and went out.

All night he wandered through the streets of St. Petersburg, without even attempting to enter any house. By morning he was tired, and sat down on the ground outside some building or other. He dozed a few minutes, then suddenly started up and walked off without looking to either side.

Soon he reached the city limits. The sleepy sentry at the gate absently noted down his surname.

He never went back to the barracks again.

11

The adjutant was a sly fellow, and told nobody about Ensign Kizhe and his own success.

Like everyone else, he had his enemies. So he told only a few people that the man who had shouted "Guards!" had been found.

But that had a strange effect on the female establishment at the palace.

The palace built by Cameron, with its slender upper columns resembling fingers playing a clavichord, had had two wings added to the main façade – wings that were rounded like the paws of a cat playing with a little mouse. In one of these two wings Nelidova, Lady in Waiting, held sway with her entourage.

Pavel Petrovich would quite often slip guiltily past the guards and make for this wing. And on one occasion the sentries had seen the Tsar running quickly out of the building, his wig awry, and a lady's shoe hurled after him and flying over his head.

Although Nelidova was only a lady in waiting, she had her own ladies in waiting.

And now, when the news reached the ladies' wing that the man who had shouted "Guards!" was found, one of Nelidova's ladies fell down in a swoon.

Like Nelidova, she was curly-haired and slim, like a shepherdess.

In the days of grandmother Elizaveta, there were brocades that crackled, silks that rustled, and unloosed nipples that peeped fearfully over them. That was the fashion then.

The Amazons who loved men's clothing, velvet nautical trains and stars at their nipples, had gone, together with her who had usurped the throne.

Nowadays women had become shepherdesses with curly locks.

And now one of them had collapsed in a brief swoon.

Once her patroness had raised her from the floor, and once she had regained consciousness, she explained: she had arranged a lovers' tryst with an officer at that very time.

However, she was unable to get away from the upper floor, and on looking out of the window she suddenly saw that the officer, all aflame with love and forgetting every caution, or perhaps not even realizing, was standing by the Tsar's very window, looking up and making signs to her.

She had waved him away, and put on an expression of horror; but her lover had misinterpreted this, and concluding that she was disgusted with him, he had sorrowfully cried out "Guards!"

At that same moment, not losing her head, she had flattened her nose with a finger and pointed downwards. The officer had been thunderstruck to see that snub-nosed sign, and hidden himself.

She hadn't seen him since. And her first tryst with him, the previous day, had been so brief that she didn't even know his name.

Now he had been found, and was being sent to Siberia.

Nelidova began to think.

Her influence was on the wane, and although she didn't like to admit it, her shoe was no longer capable of flying.

Her relations with the adjutant were chilly, and she did not want to ask him for help.

The Tsar's condition was in doubt. These days she tended to apply to a powerful man, though a civilian:

Yuri Alexandrovich Neledinsky-Meletsky.

So that was what she did: she sent him a note by a footman.

The burly footman, who had delivered many such notes, was always astonished at the beggarly style in which this powerful man lived. Meletsky was a singer and a State Secretary. He sang 'The swiftly-flowing stream', and lusted after shepherdesses. He was very short in stature, with sensual lips and bushy eyebrows. But he was also a very smart operator. Looking up at the broad-shouldered footman, he said:

"Tell her to have no anxiety. Just to wait. All this will be resolved."

But he himself was rather scared, having no idea how it was all going to be resolved. And when one of his young shepherdesses, previously called Avdotya but now Célimène, put her head round the door, he gave her a savage scowl.

Yuri Alexandrovich's household consisted for the most part of young shepherdesses.

12

The guards walked on and on.

From toll-gate to toll-gate, from guard-post to fortress, they went straight ahead, glancing anxiously at the important space that walked onwards between them.

This was not the first time that they had escorted a convict to Siberia, but they had never before taken a criminal of this sort. When they passed beyond the city limits, they had had some doubts. There was no sound of chains to be heard, and they did not need to prod the man onward with their rifle-butts. But then they thought to themselves that this was an official matter, and they had the papers with them. They talked little, for talking was forbidden.

At the first guard-post, the warder looked at them as if they were mad, and they were embarrassed. But the senior of the two showed the paper which stated that the convict was a secret individual with no visible form, and the warder busied himself and assigned them a special cell with three bunks for the night. He avoided talking to them, and made such a fuss over them that the guards couldn't help feeling how important they were.

When they came to the second guard-post, a large one, they approached it confidently, preserving an imposing silence, and the senior man simply tossed the paper onto the commander's desk. And the commander made just as much fuss and bother over them as the first one had done.

Gradually they came to realize that they were escorting an important criminal.

They got used to this, and talked meaningfully to one another, alluding to 'him' or 'it'.

And so they reached the depths of the Russian empire, along this same, straight and well-travelled Vladimirskaya highway.

And the empty space that walked patiently between them changed: sometimes it was a wind, sometimes dust, sometimes the weary, footsore heat of late summer.

13

Meanwhile there was an important order following after them, along that same Vladimirskaya highway, hurrying from guard-post to guard-post, from fortress to fortress, to catch them up.

Yuri Alexandrovich Neledinsky-Meletsky had said: wait. And he had not been wrong.

Because the great terror of Pavel Petrovich was, slowly but surely, turning into self-pity and soft-heartedness.

The Tsar would turn his back on the bushes in the gardens, which looked like animals, and walk around over the empty ground, turning his gaze towards Cameron's elegant sentiments.

He had dealt with all those governors and generals of his mother's, twisted them into a ram's horn, hidden them away on their estates, and now they were rotting there. He had been right to do that. And what had happened? A great emptiness had descended around him.

He had put up a box for complaints and messages in front of his palace, for after all it was he and no other that was the father of his nation. At first the box remained empty, and that distressed him, because a nation ought to speak to its father. Then a poison-pen letter arrived, calling him 'Daddy Snub-nose' and making threats.

He looked at himself in the mirror then.

"A snub-nose, that's what I am, my friends. Just a snub-nose," he snorted, and had the box removed.

He went on a progress through this strange land of his. He banished a governor to Siberia because the man had dared build new bridges in his lands, for the Tsar to drive over. This wasn't one of dear Mamma's progresses: everything had to be just as it was, not prettied up for him. But his nation said nothing. By the Volga, some muzhiks had gathered around him. He sent a lad to scoop up some water from the middle of the river, so that he could drink clean water.

He drank the water, and hoarsely asked the peasants:

"Here I am, drinking your water. What are you staring at?" – And emptiness descended around him.

After that he took no more journeys, and instead of the letterbox he had sturdy sentries stationed at each outpost; but he did not know if they were loyal, and he did not know whom to fear.

All around him was treachery and emptiness.

He found the secret for banishing all that, and introduced precision and total subordination. The government offices got busy. Supposedly, all he was taking was executive power; but somehow it turned out that executive power muddled up all the government offices, and what came of it was dubious treachery, emptiness, and sly obedience. He felt like a random swimmer, throwing up his empty hands in the midst of tempestuous waves – like an engraving he had once seen.

Although in fact he was the only legitimate autocrat to hold power for many a long year.

And he was oppressed by a longing to lean on his father, even a dead father. That German half-wit, murdered with a fork, who was supposed to be his father – he had him dug out of his grave, and his coffin placed alongside that of the woman who had usurped the throne. But that was done more as an act of revenge against his dead mother, during whose lifetime he had lived every minute like a man condemned to execution.

And was she really his mother?

He had some vague knowledge of the scandal surrounding his birth. He was a man without family, robbed even of his dead father, even his dead mother.

He had never thought about any of this, and if anyone had suspected him of having such thoughts, he would have had that person shot out of a cannon.

But at such moments he took pleasure in the most trivial frivolities, in the Chinese cottages of his Trianon. He would become a most sincere lover of Nature, and long for universal love, or at least the love of somebody.

This came over him in bouts, and at such times insolence would pass as sincerity, stupidity as candour, deviousness as kindness, and the Turkish orderly who polished his boots would be made a Count.

Yuri Alexandrovich, above all other sensations, could sniff out change.

He waited a week or so, and then he smelt it.

With quiet but cheerful steps, he walked round the glass screen, and abruptly told the Tsar, under the affectation of frank speaking, all that he knew about Ensign Kizhe – except, of course, for the details of that gesture about the snub nose.

At this the Tsar burst out into a barking, dog-like, hoarse, cackling guffaw, as if he was trying to frighten someone.

Yuri Alexandrovich was alarmed.

He had wanted to do a favour to Nelidova, being a family friend of hers, and incidentally to demonstrate his own importance; for as the then fashionable German proverb had it, *Umsonst ist der Tod* – only death comes free of charge. But such a guffaw could instantly demote Yuri Alexandrovich to an inferior position, or even be the instrument of his annihilation.

Perhaps it was just sarcasm?

But no, the Tsar was helpless with laughter. He held out his hand for a pen, and Yuri Alexandrovich, raising himself on tiptoe, followed the Tsar's hand as he wrote:

ENSIGN KIZHE, BANISHED TO SIBERIA, TO BE RETURNED, PROMOTED TO LIEUTENANT, AND MARRIED TO THAT LADY IN WAITING.

After which the Tsar set to walking around the room, full of enthusiasm.

He clapped his hands and struck up his favourite song, whistling and singing:

"My little clump of fir-trees,

My thick little clump of birch-trees…"

And Yuri Alexandrovich joined in, in his thin and ever so quiet voice:

"Lyushenki-lyuli."

14

A dog that's been badly bitten likes to go out into the fields and dose itself with bitter herbs.

Lieutenant Sinyukhayev was walking from St. Petersburg to Gatchina. He was going to see his father – not to ask for help, but just like that, perhaps because he wanted to check whether his father existed at Gatchina, or whether perhaps he didn't exist. He said nothing in reply to his father's greeting, simply looked around, and was on the point of departing, like a man who feels shy or even coy.

But the doctor, seeing the deficiencies in his clothing, sat him down and started asking him questions.

"Have you lost money at cards, or done something you shouldn't?"

"I'm not alive," replied the lieutenant abruptly.

The doctor felt his pulse, said something about leeches, and went on asking questions.

When he heard about his son's blunder, he became agitated, spent a whole hour writing down and copying out a petition, made his son sign it, and next day went to see Baron Arakcheyev so as to have the petition delivered along with the daily report. However, he didn't dare keep his son at home, so he admitted him to the hospital, and on the board above his bed he wrote:

Mors occasional

Accidental death

15

Baron Arakcheyev worried about the notion of of the state. That made his character difficult to define. He was elusive.

The Baron did not bear grudges, and sometimes he was even gracious. When he heard some affecting story, he would burst into tears like a child, and when he walked round the garden, he would give the garden-girl a kopek. Afterwards, noticing that the garden paths hadn't been properly swept, he would have the girl thrashed with a cane. When the punishment was done, he would give her a five-kopek piece.

In the presence of the Tsar, he felt a sense of weakness that resembled love.

He loved cleanliness; that was the symbol of his personality. But it was precisely when he found deficiencies in cleanliness and order that he was content; and if none were found, he was secretly annoyed. Instead of a hot roast, he always ate salted meat.

He was as absent-minded as a philosopher. Indeed, learned Germans found that his eyes resembled those of the philosopher Kant, well known in Germany at the time: they had a moist, indeterminate colour, and were covered by a transparent film. But the Baron was offended when someone mentioned this resemblance to him.

Not only was he stingy, he also loved making a show, and displaying everything to best effect. For this purpose, he would enter into the most finicking domestic details.

He would sit and study plans for oratories, medals, icons, or dinner menus. He was attracted to circles, ellipses and lines which intersected like the lashes of a three-tailed whip, creating a structure which could deceive the eye. And he liked deceiving his visitors, or deceiving the Tsar and pretending not to notice when anyone was plotting to deceive him in turn. But deceiving him, of course, was difficult.

He kept a detailed inventory of the belongings of all his staff, from his personal valet to the kitchen-boy, and he checked over all the hospital inventories.

When organizing the hospital where Lieutenant Sinyukhayev's father worked, the Baron personally directed how the beds were to be arranged, where benches should stand, where the orderly's desk should go, and even what his quill pen should look like – bare, with no barb, resembling a Roman *calamus* – a reed. Having a pen with a barb would earn a doctor's assistant five lashes with the cane.

The notion of the Roman state worried Baron Arakcheyev.

Hence he listened absently to Doctor Sinyukhayev's tale, and it was not until the doctor handed over his petition that he carefully read it through, and reprimanded the doctor because the paper was illegibly signed.

The doctor apologized and explained that his son's hand had been shaking.

"Aha! Well there you are, my friend!" replied the baron with satisfaction. "Even his hand shakes."

Then, looking at the doctor, he asked him:

"When did the death occur?"

"June the fifteenth," replied the doctor, somewhat taken aback.

"June the fifteenth," drawled the baron, thinking about it. "June the fifteenth... And today's already the seventeenth," he suddenly snapped at the doctor. "Wherever has the dead man been these two days?"

Then he scowled at the doctor, glanced sourly at the petition, and said:

"What a way to carry on! Now goodbye, my man, get along with you."

16

Meletsky, singer and State Secretary, threw himself into whatever he did, took risks and often won, because he saw everything in enchanting colours, like Cameron's; but his wins gave way to losses, as in a game of Quadrille.

Baron Arakcheyev behaved differently. He never took risks, and never vouched for anything. On the contrary: in his reports to the Tsar, he would point out instances of abuse (thus, and thus!) and ask permission to take the necessary preventive measures.

Meletsky risked belittlement; the baron belittled himself. But the winnings that gleamed in the distance were big ones, as in the game of Faro.

He dispassionately informed the Tsar that the dead lieutenant Sinyukhayev had presented himself at Gatchina, where he had been put in the hospital.

And that he had claimed to be alive, and submitted a petition to be reinstated on the registers. Which petition was here presented to the Tsar with a request for further instructions. By presenting this paper, he wished to demonstrate his dutiful obedience, like an assiduous bailiff who consults his master on every point.

The answers quickly followed – one to the petition, and one to Baron Arakcheyev in person.

The petition was overwritten with the following decision:

PETITION OF ERSTWHILE LIEUTENANT SINYUKHAYEV, DELETED FROM THE REGISTER BY REASON OF DEATH, TO BE DENIED FOR THE ABOVE REASON.

And a note was delivered to Baron Arakcheyev:

BARON ARAKCHEYEV, SIR,

I AM ASTONISHED THAT YOU, POSSESSING A GENERAL'S RANK, DO NOT KNOW THE REGULATIONS, BUT HAVE ADDRESSED DIRECTLY TO ME THE PETITION OF DECEASED LIEUTENANT SINYUKHAYEV, WHO FURTHERMORE IS NOT FROM YOUR REGIMENT, A PETITION WHICH SHOULD IN THE FIRST INSTANCE HAVE BEEN CONVEYED DIRECTLY TO THE OFFICE OF THIS LIEUTENANT'S REGIMENT, WITHOUT BURDENING ME PERSONALLY WITH A PETITION OF THIS SORT.

HOWEVER, YOU HAVE MY GOOD WISHES.

PAVEL

The note did not say 'my good wishes, as ever'.

And Arakcheyev burst into tears, for he absolutely hated being told off. He went personally to the hospital and gave orders for the dead lieutenant to be expelled forthwith, and for underclothes to be issued to him; but the officer's uniform registered to him to be retained.

17

When Lieutenant Kizhe returned from Siberia, many people already knew about him. He was that same lieutenant who had called out 'Guards!' under the Tsar's window, and who had been punished and sent to Siberia, and then pardoned and promoted to full lieutenant. Those were the absolutely definite facts of his life.

His commanding officer no longer felt at all uncomfortable with him; he simply detailed him off to guard duty one day, or other duties on another. When the regiment was despatched to camp for manoeuvres, the lieutenant went along too. He was a good officer, for he could not be implicated in any wrongdoing.

The lady in waiting whose brief swoon had saved him was at first pleased at the thought that she was to be united with her sudden lover. She placed a patch on her cheek and tightened her corset lacing, which would not meet. Then, in church, she noticed that she was standing on her own, and that an adjutant was holding up the bridegroom's wreath over the empty place beside her. She was about to faint away once more, but as she was keeping her eyes lowered and looking at her waist, she changed her mind. The somewhat mysterious nature of a ceremony at which no bridegroom was present appealed to many people there.

And some time later a son was born to Lieutenant Kizhe, who was said to resemble him.

The Tsar forgot about him. He was a busy man.

Quick-witted Nelidova was dismissed, and her place was taken by plump Gagarina.

Cameron, the Swiss chalets, the whole of Pavlovskoye itself, were forgotten. Squat, soldierly St. Petersburg lay in red-brick neatness. Suvorov, whom the Tsar disliked but put up with, because Suvorov was an enemy of the late Potemkin, became alarmed in his rustic solitude. A campaign was imminent, because the Tsar had plans. There were many such plans, and one of them would often leap-frog another. Pavel Petrovich spread out sideways and his figure sagged. His face became brick-red. Suvorov fell out of favour again. The Tsar laughed more and more rarely.

Riffling through the regimental registers, he once came across the name of Lieutenant Kizhe, and promoted him to captain; and later on, made him a colonel. The lieutenant was a good officer. Then the Tsar forgot him again.

Colonel Kizhe's life passed unnoticed, and everyone got used to that.

At home he had his own office, in the barracks he had his own room, and occasionally people brought along reports or orders, but showed no particular surprise at the colonel's absence.

He was already in command of a regiment.

Happiest of all was the lady in waiting, as she occupied their enormous double bed.

Her husband was getting on in his career, sleeping was comfortable, and their son was growing up. Sometimes the colonel's marital bed was warmed by a lieutenant, a captain or a civilian. That was something that happened in many colonels' beds in St. Petersburg, while their owners were away on a campaign.

Once, while an exhausted lover was sleeping, she heard something creak in the next room. Then it creaked again. No question about it, it was the floorboards drying out. But she instantly shook the sleeping man awake, chased him away, and threw his clothes out after him.

When she had calmed down, she laughed at herself.

But that, too, was something that happened in many colonels' homes.

18

The peasants smelt of the wind, their women smelt of smoke.

Lieutenant Sinyukhayev looked no one in the face; he told people apart by their smell.

It was by smell that he found a place to sleep; he tried to sleep under trees, because under a tree the rain didn't wet one so badly.

He walked on, stopping nowhere.

He passed through villages of Finnish-speaking peasants the way a stone flicked by a boy skims over a river – barely touching. Occasionally one of those

Finnish women would give him some milk. He drank it standing up, and walked on. The children fell silent, their faces gleaming with whitish slime. The village closed up behind him.

His gait had not changed much. Walking had made it looser, but that crumbly, loose, almost toy-like gait was still an officer's military gait.

He took no account of the direction he was going. But his direction could be identified. Deviating this way and that, making zig-zags like the lightnings painted on pictures of the Great Flood, he described circles, and those circles gradually narrowed down.

A year passed, before the circle contracted into a single point and he entered St. Petersburg. Entering it, he walked round it from one end to the other.

Then he began circling within the city, and sometimes he walked the same circle again and again for weeks.

He walked quickly, keeping to his loose military gait, his arms and legs seeming to dangle from his sides.

The shopkeepers loathed him.

When he happened to walk along Gostiny Ryad (Traders' Row), they shouted after him:

"Come back yesterday!"

"Play it backwards!"

They said he brought bad luck. The bun-selling women tried to buy off his evil eye by silently agreeing to give him a bun each.

The street urchins, who throughout history have been brilliant at detecting weakness, ran after him shouting:

"The hanged man!"

19

In St. Petersburg, the sentries around Pavel Petrovich's fortress shouted:

"The Tsar is sleeping!"

The cry was taken up by the guards with their halberds at the crossroads:

"The Tsar is sleeping!"

And the cry went like a wind, causing the shops to shut one after another, while walkers went into hiding in their homes. It meant evening.

On Isaakievsky Square, the crowds of peasants dressed in sackcloth who had been forced out of their villages to come and work, put out their bonfires and lay down on the earth where they stood, covering themselves with rags.

When the guards with their halberds had called out "The Tsar is sleeping!", they went to sleep themselves. On the Petropavlovsky fortress a sentry paced back and forth like clockwork. In a certain tavern on the outskirts of town, a Cossack lad wearing a sash of bast sat with a coachman, drinking the Tsar's wine.

"Daddy Snub-nose will be done for soon," said the coachman. "I've had important gentry in my cab."

The drawbridge of the fortress was raised, and Pavel Petrovich looked out of his window.

He was safe for now, on his island.

But in the palace there were whispers and glances, which he understood; and the people he encountered on the streets fell down on their knees before his horse with strange expressions on their faces.

They were supposed to do that, but now the people fell down in the mud in a different way from before. They fell too suddenly. The horse was a tall one, and he swayed in his saddle. He reigned too briskly. The fortress was inadequately defended, too spacious. He needed to choose a smaller room. However, Pavel Petrovich couldn't do that – someone would have noticed at once. "Ought to hide in a snuff-box," thought the Tsar, taking snuff. He didn't light his candle. No point giving himself away. He stood in the darkness, in nothing but his shift. By the window, he counted people. Made substitutions. Deleted Bennigsen from his memory, and introduced Olsufyev. The list didn't work out.

"My own count is missing," he said.

"Arakcheyev's stupid" he said quietly.

"...*la vague incertitude* with which he tries to please me... the sentry could hardly be seen at the drawbridge."

"Ought to..." said Pavel Petrovich, as was his habit. He drummed his fingertips on his snuffbox.

"Ought to..." he recalled, and drummed his fingertips, and suddenly stopped. Everything that ought to be done had been done long ago, and had turned out not to be enough.

"Ought to lock up Alexander Pavlovich," he said hurriedly, and waved the thought aside.

"Ought to... What ought to be done?"

He lay down, and darted under his blanket; everything he did, he did quickly. And fell fast asleep.

At seven in the morning he woke with a start, and remembered: he ought to find a plain, modest man to serve him, a man totally devoted to him; and get rid of everyone else.

Then he fell asleep again.

20

In the morning Pavel Petrovich looked over the day's orders. Colonel Kizhe was summarily promoted to general. He had been a colonel who never coveted estates, never climbed in society by hanging on an uncle's coat-tails, wasn't a windbag or a fop. He carried out his duties without grumbling or attracting attention.

Pavel Petrovich demanded his service record. He paused over a paper that reported that the colonel, when an ensign, had been exiled to Siberia for calling out 'Guards!' under the Tsar's window. The Tsar recalled something from the mists of his memory, and smiled. There had been a bit of a love intrigue mixed up in that.

He could have done with someone, now, who would call out 'Guards!' under his window, at the right moment. He granted General Kizhe a country estate and a thousand souls.

That same evening, General Kizhe's name surfaced again. He was being talked about. Someone had heard the Tsar say to Count Pahlen, with a smile such as had not been seen for a long time, "Don't be too quick to saddle him with a division. He's needed for more important work."

No one but Bennigsen wanted to admit that they knew nothing about the general. Pahlen screwed up his eyes.

Alexander Lvovich Naryshkin, Master of the Tsar's Bedchamber, remembered the general:

"Yes indeed, Colonel Kizhe… I remember. He had a thing with Sandunova…"

"On manoeuvres at Krasnoe…"

"If I remember rightly, he's related to Olsufyev, Fedor Yakovlevich…"

"He's no relation of Olsufyev's, count. Colonel Kizhe is from France. His father was beheaded by the rabble at Toulon."

21

Events moved swiftly. General Kizhe was summoned to attend the Tsar. That same day the Tsar was informed that the general was gravely ill.

He grunted with vexation and twisted a button off Pahlen's tunic. Pahlen had brought the news.

"Get him sent to hospital and cured. And if they don't cure him, sir…"

One of the Tsar's lackeys visited the hospital twice a day to find out how the General was.

In a great ward, behind tightly closed doors, the doctors bustled about, trembling like sick men themselves.

On the third evening, General Kizhe passed away.

Pavel Petrovich wasn't angry any longer. He looked morosely at everyone and went off to his quarters.

22

General Kizhe's funeral was long remembered in St. Petersburg, and certain writers of memoirs have recorded the details.

The regiment marched with banners furled. Thirty palace coaches, full and empty, swayed along behind them. Such was the Tsar's wish. The General's medals were borne on cushions.

The General's wife followed the massive black coffin, leading her son by the hand.

She was weeping.

As the procession made its way past Pavel Petrovich's fortress, he and an attendant slowly rode out onto the drawbridge to watch it pass, and raised his drawn sword.

"My best people are dying."

Then he waited for the palace coaches to drive by, following them with his eyes, and said:

"Sic transit gloria mundi."

23

And so General Kizhe was buried, having performed everything in his life that he could have done; he died, replete with all the qualities of youth, a love-affair, punishment and exile, years of service, a family, the sudden favour of the Tsar, and the envy of those at court.

His name is recorded in the *Saint Petersburg Necropolis*, and certain historians mention him in passing.

The *Saint Petersburg Necropolis* makes no mention of the late Lieutenant Sinyukhayev.

He has disappeared without trace, crumbled into dust, into chaff, as if he had never existed.

And Pavel Petrovich died in March of the same year as General Kizhe – according to official accounts, of apoplexy.